We are deeply grateful to all the generous people
who helped shape this story,
reflecting the many cultures, identities, and perspectives
offered in Maya's journey.

The brave little girl who inspired this fictional story
is a beautiful blend of her Caribbean and American parents,
a heritage that reaches back
to Africa, Europe and the Americas, representing multiple threads
of the extraordinary tapestry of humanity.

Mermaid Dreams is dedicated to all the world's children
who dare to dream.

D1294355

Mermaid Dreams

by
Janet Lucy

illustrated by
Colleen McCarthy-Evans

Maya dreams
of being a mermaid.

Her long dark hair hangs
in silky strands
down her back
nearly reaching the top
of her favorite skirt -
the one her mama made
with seven tiers of turquoise net.

Maya dances
to Caribbean mermaid music
and feels the skirt's waves
on her strong agile legs.

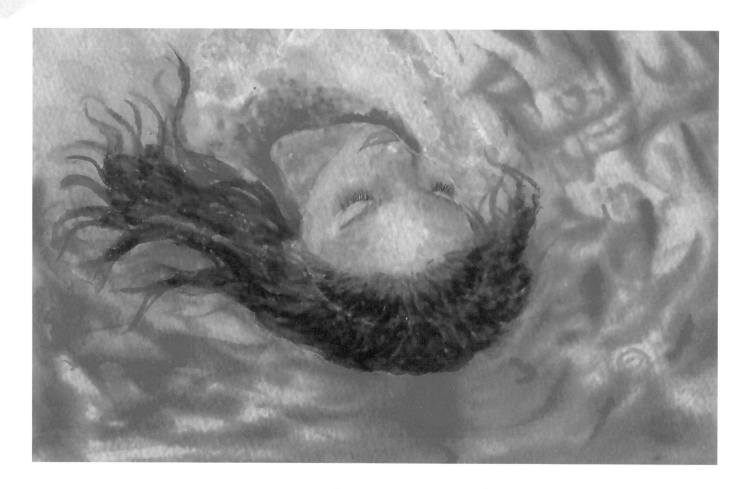

Maya loves the pool at the park
where she takes swim lessons
all summer long.
Her stroke is sure and strong
from one side to the other.
She can float on her back forever.

She holds her breath
and dives for shiny coins
in the shallow and deep water.

At the end of the summer
Maya asks,
"Mama can you sign me up
for more swim lessons?
I can hold my breath
but I still need to come up for air.
I can't breathe underwater yet."

Maya believes
if she could breathe
underwater like a mermaid,
she would be safe beneath the waves
that frighten her.

Maya's mama is from an island
in the Caribbean Sea.

Maya loves to hear her mama's stories
of soft white sandy beaches covered in shells,
swimming with shimmering colorful fish
in warm clear turquoise water,
and the rhythm of gentle waves
that lulled her to sleep.

Where Maya lives on the coast of California,
the ocean is colder.
The waves look so big to her
and crash so loud!

Maya stands on the shore,
wades in up to her ankles
and watches a wave rise up.

She takes a brave breath and a tiny step forward,
then jumps back.

She asks Mama,
"Will they swallow me up?"

At night Maya has frightening dreams
of waves, tall as towers, taking over the land.
Maya is afraid to go to sleep.

One night before bed, Maya says,
"Mama, tell me again
about my namesake, Yemaya."

Mama carries Maya to her bed,
covered in a turquoise comforter,
and climbs in with her.

As she tells Maya the story,
Mama twists the many strands and colors
of Maya's hair
into long mermaid curls.

*"In the beginning
Yemaya was an African Orisha,
a river spirit of the Yoruba people.*

*She swam in the rivers and streams,
slipping between rocks and smooth stones,
playing with her children
in schools of fish."*

*"When her people were enslaved
and forced to leave Africa,
Yemaya followed them across the oceans,
offering comfort alongside the ships.*

*She became the Goddess of the Ocean
with many names -
Mother Ocean, Mother of Water,
and Mama Watta in Africa.*

*Yemaya is at home in the seven oceans,
where she protects all the creatures of the sea,
especially children who love to swim."*

Mama smiles at Maya.

*"One day while Yemaya was swimming
with the peaceful sea turtles,
she sensed turmoil in the water."*

*"The ocean was growing dark
and rising up into a monstrous wave."*

"That's like my dream!"
Maya exclaims, eyes wide open.
Mama pulls her close.

"Fortunately," Mama assures her ...

"Yemaya swam swiftly to the surface
where she saw the people on shore
running in fear
as the huge mountain of water
came rushing toward them.

Yemaya took a deep breath
then blew powerfully into her conch shell,
commanding the wave to stop.

Yemaya was able to calm the fury of the sea
just in time."

23

"The giant wave changed shape
and settled onto the shore.

The water gently receded,
leaving Yemaya's gifts -
shells and glistening pearls
on the sand.

The ocean was calm again."

"According to her legend," Mama continues,
"one of Yemaya's first gifts to humans
was a sea shell
in which her voice could always be heard."

Mama pauses and opens her palms.

"This is a gift my mother gave me,
one of the spiral shells
Yemaya once left on the sand
on our island."

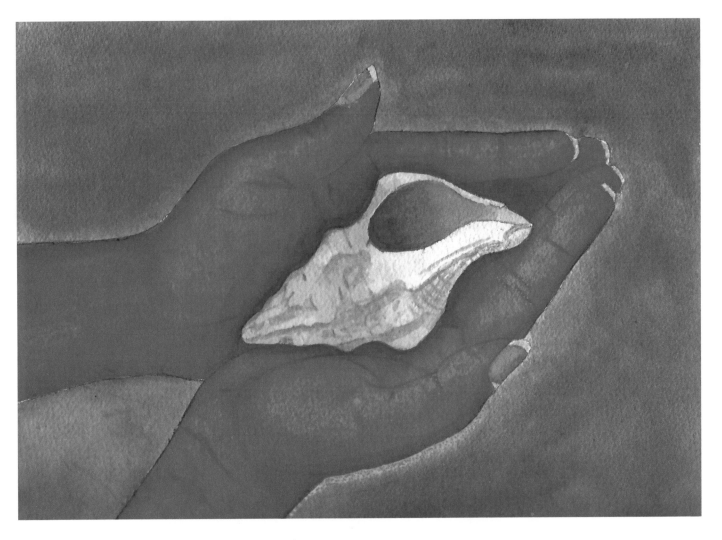

"If you hold it to your ear,
you can hear Yemaya's voice,
the vibration of the sea.
Through this shell
she also sings children to sleep."

"You see, Yemaya is a mermaid,
who not only lives in the sea,
she also swims through dreams
and comforts children while they sleep."

Maya holds the shell to her ear.

Her body relaxes,
and though her eyes are shining,
her eyelids begin to flutter.

"I'm ready to go to sleep," Maya tells Mama,
as she drifts off dreamily.

"Good evening, dear one. Did you call to me?
I heard the sweetest voice whisper my name."

Maya's eyes open wide in wonder
as she meets Yemaya in her dream.

"Yes," she replies softly.

"Would you like to go on a magical journey
and see the beauty beneath the sea?"

"I can't swim underwater yet
without holding my breath."

"You can in your dreams,"
Yemaya assures her, extending her hand.
"Come with me."

Maya reaches for Yemaya's hand.

As they descend
into the dreamy waters together,
Yemaya guides Maya through the depths.

Maya marvels at the beauty
all around them.

Colorful fish flutter by.
Giant clam shells open like fans.

Pearls hang among strands of seaweed.
Sand-dollars like moons
are scattered on the sandy floor.

At the end of the journey
Yemaya tucks Maya into a clam bed,
a soft sea sponge beneath her head.

Maya smiles and closes her eyes.

"Good night, dear one.
Call me anytime.
I'm always nearby in your dreams
and in the sea ..."

"And remember, when you are having scary dreams,
you have the power
to re-imagine your dreams
and change the way they end,"
Yemaya assures Maya, as gentle bubbles rise.

The next morning is sunny and bright.
Maya stretches her long legs
beneath her blanket.

She climbs out of bed,
puts on her sparkling blue bathing suit,
and fastens her favorite cowrie shell bracelet
around her wrist.

"Can we go to the beach today?"
Maya asks Mama.

"Yes, of course," Mama laughs,
"It looks like you're ready to go."

Mama and Maya
walk to the shore,
where they wade out together
into the cool blue water.

As a new wave rises up overhead,
Maya smiles at Mama,
takes a deep breath
and dives through.

"I did it!" Maya shouts,
as she breaks through the wave.

Mermaid Dreams ~ Discussion Guide & Activities

Dear Parents, Grandparents, Teachers and Friends,

Thank you for reading *Mermaid Dreams* to the children in your lives. The following are some ideas for continuing a discussion about the themes in the book. Consider asking children any of these questions. For younger children keep them simple!

1. What stood out for you in the story? What did you like about *Mermaid Dreams*?

2. What are some things you know about Maya? Do you see any ways in which you and Maya are alike?

3. What does Maya want to do that she has never done before? What would you like to do you have not yet done?

4. Maya's namesake is Yemaya. Who is Yemaya and why do you think Maya was named after her? Are you named after someone? If so, do you know why?

5. Maya's seven tiered skirt is symbolic of the Goddess Yemaya and the ocean. What do you imagine it represents?

6. What do you think is magical about mermaids?

7. Dreaming of extraordinary or magical powers is natural. What magical power do you wish you had? What is your "super power," or what would you like it to be? How might a "super power" help you in your life?

8. There are many kinds of dreams. Nighttime dreams, daydreams, and dreams that are hopes or wishes. What kinds of dreams do you have? What kinds of dreams do you remember?

9. At the end of the underwater dream journey Yemaya reminds Maya she has the power to change the ending of her scary dreams. Have you ever had a dream that you wished you could change?

10. Yemaya uses the giant conch shell like a voice to amplify her power to stop the wave. When would you use your powerful voice?

11. Yemaya's small spiral shell is symbolic of listening to a wise inner voice. How do you listen to your inner voice?

12. In the beginning Yemaya was an Orisha from West Africa. Can you find West Africa on a map? What else can you find out about the people of Yoruba?

13. In Yemaya's legend she became the Goddess of the Ocean when she followed her people who were taken from their homeland in Africa, enslaved and sold in the Americas. Throughout history people have treated others unfairly and cruelly because of their skin color, culture and race, and where they come from and the language they speak. When you see people being treated unfairly, how can you offer support? How can you offer respect and understanding when you meet someone who seems different from you? When you notice someone isn't being included, what can you do?

14. At the end of the story Maya wears her favorite cowrie shell bracelet to the beach. Do you have something that you wear or keep with you to make you feel courageous, strong, or safe?

15. How does Maya's story end? How does she find courage? Have you ever overcome a fear and felt like Maya?

Mermaid Dreams Activities:
1. On the first page of *Mermaid Dreams*, Maya has a drawing of a mermaid on the wall. Invite children to draw or create a mermaid like Maya did. Mixed media is fun, too!

2. Find some Caribbean or African music for children to listen or dance to. For starters, try searching the internet for *Caribbean* music genres, as well as *Igbo* or *Yoruba* music.

3. Encourage children to draw pictures of their dreams and tell their story. If they are scary dreams, they might try giving them a new ending.

4. Prompt children to write or tell "My dream is ..." about a wish, hope, or dream.

5. Yemaya took a deep breath before blowing into her conch shell to calm the large wave. Teach children to practice long, deep breathing into their bellies to experience a calming effect.

6. If you can visit a beach, invite children to look for a spiral shell like Maya's, and listen for Yemaya's voice. Though spiral shells are some of the most magical shells you can find, today we're more aware of the importance of leaving shells on the beach. Hermit crabs (and other sea creatures) use them as their home. As hermit crabs grow, they must move into ever larger shells. So even if the shell you find is empty, it is waiting for its next inhabitant. If you find a spiral shell, please leave it on the sand after listening to Yemaya's voice. *Maya will return Yemaya's gift to the sea, and carry her voice inside her.*

Author's Note ~ Inspiration for *Mermaid Dreams*

My first book, *Moon Mother, Moon Daughter ~ Myths and Rituals that Celebrate a Girl's Coming of Age*, illuminated the worldwide moon goddess culture. Since its publication in 2002, the ancient Black Madonnas have been whispering to me, inspiring a new quest— to contribute to the remembering and honoring of the dark mother goddesses and share their love and wisdom.

It's been my dream to author a children's book about a mermaid and goddess of color, to help expand the mosaic of mermaid imagery, so that more children can recognize themselves in this magical archetype.

The inspiration for *Mermaid Dreams* came first from my muse, the real life "Maya," who offered the initial ideas for the book—a little girl who loves to swim, dreams of being a mermaid, and had frightening dreams at night. These concepts are universal—dreams and fears of children and adults alike.

Yemaya slipped into my reverie early one winter morning as I sat in the pre-dawn darkness, facing the horizon, awaiting the first light. I am grateful and honored that Yemaya, the Goddess of the Ocean, offered her luminous myth to weave into Maya's dream. I feel strongly that we all have divine assistants and protectors available, sometimes simply waiting for the invitation to enter our daily lives and nighttime dreams, just as Yemaya does for Maya in *Mermaid Dreams*.

The watercolor illustrations by Colleen McCarthy-Evans give this book the magic only her heart and hands could divine. I'm grateful for our continuous collaboration, as well as that of Erika Römer, who has also generously offered inspiration and wisdom throughout the retelling of the stories of Maya and Yemaya. I share them here with the deepest respect.

Sources & Resources

If you'd like to explore similar stories or learn more about the themes, here are a few "Sources and Resources" we recommend at Seven Seas Press.

Children's Books:

The Book of Goddesses by Kris Waldherr (February 1996)

Julian Is a Mermaid by Jessica Love (April 2018)

Jabari Jumps by Gaia Cornwall (May 2017)

Tar Beach by Faith Ringgold (December 1996)

Aunt Harriet's Underground Railroad in the Sky by Faith Ringgold (December 1995)

Henry's Freedom Box: A True Story from the Underground Railroad by Ellen Levine and Kadir Nelson (December 2006)

Podcast:

lourdesviado.com/112-the-wisdom-of-mermaid-dreams/
Listen to an interview with author, Janet Lucy, discuss *Mermaid Dreams* with Dr. Lourdes Viado, PhD, MFT, Jungian psychotherapist & host of the *Women In-Depth* podcast

Websites:

janetlucyink.com
sevenseaspress.org

AUTHOR - Janet Lucy, MA, is an award-winning writer and poet, and author of *Moon Mother, Moon Daughter - Myths and Rituals that Celebrate a Girl's Coming of Age* and *The Three Sunflowers/Los Tres Girasoles.* Janet is the Director of Women's Creative Network in Santa Barbara, California, where she is a teacher, therapist/consultant, facilitates women's writing groups and leads international retreats. She has lived in Mexico, Costa Rica and Italy, connecting with the Divine Feminine in all her glorious guises and cultural richness. Janet is the mother of two radiant daughters.

ILLUSTRATOR - Colleen McCarthy-Evans is an award-winning writer and illustrator *(The Little Blue Dragon/La Dragoncita Azul* and *The Three Sunflowers/Los Tres Girasoles)* and board game inventor. She's a co-founder and former Director of Operations of the Santa Barbara Charter School (est. 1993), whose mission is to teach Conflict Resolution along with Academics and the Arts. She lives in Santa Barbara, California with her husband and their dogs, loves to practice and teach Kundalini Yoga, and enjoys being in and out of the garden with her two grown sons, extended family and friends.

Additional offerings from the Author and Illustrator:

More praise for *Mermaid Dreams* from Psychologists, Teachers, and Parents:

"In *Mermaid Dreams*, Janet Lucy tells the poignant story of Maya, a little girl who is afraid of the ocean - and her namesake Yemaya, the Goddess of the Ocean. But beneath the surface of Maya's story is a reminder to the souls of women everywhere. Janet's writing and Colleen McCarthy-Evans' vivid illustrations call us inward to the deep wisdom within; reminding us of the significance of our dreams; of the value of going within; to pay attention to our intuition; to listen to our inner voice; and to express ourselves authentically and powerfully."
~ Lourdes Viado
PhD, MFT, Jungian psychotherapist & host of the *Women In-Depth* podcast

"*Mermaid Dreams* is a gem! Beautifully written and illustrated; it's a story for us all! Janet Lucy's choice of Yemaya, a mythical goddess/mermaid of color, is refreshingly powerful in challenging the blonde, blue-eyed mermaid stereotype, which invites the sea and all its magic to each of us, no matter the color of one's skin. Using ancient storytelling, *Mermaid Dreams* gently guides and encourages us to explore our dream worlds as they may be a vessel in changing one's own story and life. The Discussion Guide and Activities at the end of the book adds volumes to this insightful, wise, and engaging story. A real treasure for children, families, teachers, and counselors."
~ Kristy Raihn
MA, Clinical Psychology, mother, lover of the sea, community programs creator in Costa Rica

"A magical story that gives voice to scary dreams and explores the power to change the ending. The Discussion Questions and Activities at the end of the book create many opportunities to expand conversations about myths, dreams and personal power. Plus, who doesn't wish to be a mermaid?"
~ Terri Allison
co-author, *Moon Mother, Moon Daughter ~ Myths and Rituals that Celebrate a Girl's Coming of Age*

And from children:

" ... It made me feel brave." **~ age 7**

" ... It made me feel calm and happy." **~ age 6**

" ... I learned to believe in myself." **~ age 6**

" ... It made me feel happy because she wasn't scared anymore." **~ age 7**

" ... You can do anything in your dreams." **~ age 7**

" ... I want to go to the beach!" **~ age 6**